COUNTRY INSIGHTS

JAPAN

Nick Bornoff

RSVP
RAINTREE
STECK-VAUGHN
PUBLISHERS
The Steck-Vaughn Company

Austin, Texas

COUNTRY INSIGHTS

BRAZIL • CHINA • FRANCE • JAMAICA • JAPAN • KENYA • MEXICO • PAKISTAN

GUIDE TO THIS BOOK

As well as telling you about the whole of Japan, this book looks closely at the city of Okazaki and the village of Narai.

 This city symbol will appear at the top of the page and information boxes each time Okazaki is discussed.

 This rural symbol will appear each time Narai is discussed.

Title page: Catching some early summer sun on Shikoku Island

Contents page: Mount Fuji, on the main island of Honshu, is Japan's highest mountain. It is also a sleeping volcano, which last erupted in 1707. Mount Fuji is seen as sacred by many Japanese.

Published by Raintree Steck-Vaughn Publishers, an imprint of Steck-Vaughn Company

Library of Congress Cataloging-in-Publication Data
Bornoff, Nick.
Japan / Nick Bornoff.
      p.   cm.—(Country insights)
Includes bibliographical references and index.
Summary: Introduces aspects of the geography, social structure, and economy of the Asian island nation of Japan.
ISBN 0-8172-4786-6
1. Japan—Juvenile literature.
[1. Japan.]
I. Title. II. Series.
DS806.B59 1997
952—dc20   96-27537

Printed in Italy. Bound in the United States.
1 2 3 4 5 6 7 8 9 0 0 01 00 99 98 97

Contents

Introducing Japan 4

Landscape and Climate 10

Home Life 16

Japan at Work 22

Going to School 28

Japan at Play 34

The Future 40

Glossary 46

Further Information 47

Index 48

興陽製紙

Introducing Japan

Japan lies off the east coast of mainland Asia and consists of the four main islands of Hokkaido, Honshu, Shikoku, and Kyushu. There are also over 3,000 smaller islands. These are spread over a distance of 1,500 miles, from the isolated islands north of Hokkaido in the northeast to the sunny Ryukyu group in the south. The capital, Tokyo, is on the main island of Honshu.

The first people of Japan probably came from Siberia. Later, over many centuries, settlers arrived from Korea and China. These were the ancestors of the modern Japanese. Beginning with rice farming, the settlers introduced Chinese civilization, including writing, science, art, architecture, and the Buddhist religion. From this mixed background, the Japanese developed a culture of their own.

The Japanese balance ancient and modern ways of life together. They believe in Shinto, a religion that dates back to prehistoric times. When the Buddhist religion arrived, 1,300 years ago, the two religions began to be practiced side by side. Today, many colorful festivals all over the country celebrate the religion of Shinto.

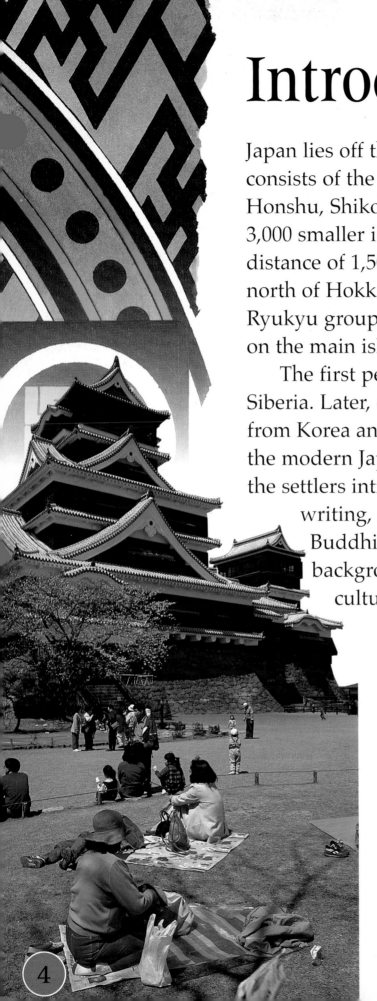

Kumamoto Castle is one of many old samurai fortresses dotted throughout Japan.

Kyoto's three-day Gion Matsuri festival ▶ *attracts hundreds of thousands of people. One of the highlights of the festival is a parade of floats through the city streets.*

JAPAN	
Total land area:	145,800 sq. mi.
Population:	125.9 million
Capital:	Tokyo
Highest mountain:	Mt. Fuji, 12,400 ft.
Currency:	Yen

Source: *Facts and Figures Japan* (Foreign Press Center, 1995)

By 1900, Japan had become the most advanced nation in Asia. After World War II (1939–1945), which devastated the country, Japan had to rebuild its cities and industries. From the 1950s, however, Japan began to grow into one of the wealthiest and most technologically advanced countries in the world. Today, Japan is the world leader in the production of cars, machinery, and electronics, and its wealth is second only to the United States.

This book will take ▶ *you to the city of Okazaki and the village of Narai, as well as the rest of Japan. You can find these places on the map.*

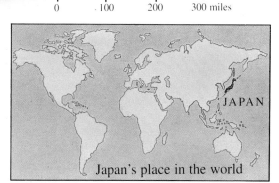

HOKKAIDO

SEA OF JAPAN

HONSHU

JAPANESE ALPS

Narai
Kiso
Mt. Fuji
Tokyo
Kyoto
Nagoya
Yokohama
Kobe
Okazaki

PACIFIC OCEAN

SHIKOKU

KYUSHU

EAST CHINA SEA

N

RYUKYU ISLANDS

OKINAWA

0	100	200	300	400	500 km
0		100		200	300 miles

JAPAN

Japan's place in the world

THE CITY OF OKAZAKI

Okazaki is a thriving city of 320,000 residents that lies near the southeast coast of the main island of Honshu. It is about 50 miles from the busy city of Nagoya, the regional capital.

People have lived in Okazaki since prehistoric times. The city is famous for being the birthplace of Tokugawa Ieyasu (1542–1610), who was the greatest of all the shoguns, or samurai rulers. Shoguns, who were originally warriors, were military leaders who ruled Japan from 1603 to 1868. Ieyasu was an important shogun because he united Japan after 500 years of civil war. He then began building roads between the country's major cities. Okazaki became an important city along the main road between what is now Tokyo in the east and Kyoto in the west. This road was called the Tokaido. Ieyasu built the basis of the main road system still in use in Japan.

Okazaki during rush hour. This busy main street is part of the national expressway to Nagoya.

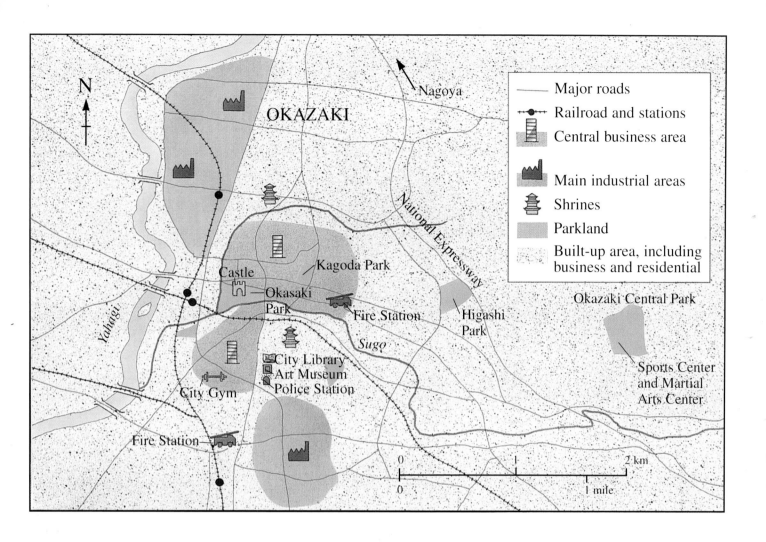

Due to Japan's industrialization Okazaki's population has tripled since 1945. The city was badly damaged during the war and then rebuilt, so it is now a modern city with only a few old temples left standing. Yet despite its modern buildings and booming industries, Okazaki remains a very traditional city. There are still a large number of traditional crafts and industries that are hundreds of years old in the city. Okazaki's ability to mix old traditions with new technologies successfully makes this city typically Japanese.

Fermented soybeans are made into miso paste. Miso is still prepared in Okazaki from methods that are centuries old.

THE VILLAGE OF NARAI

Narai is a sleepy village that lies in the valley of the Kiso River. It has a population of only a few hundred people. This beautiful area is famous for its mountains, rivers, forests, and waterfalls. Narai lies on an old mountain road, called the Nakasendo, which was once an alternative route between the cities of Edo (modern-day Tokyo) and Kyoto.

Like Okazaki, Narai used to be an important point along a major road. In 1911, however, a railroad was built to connect the towns along the way, and the Nakasendo fell into disuse. As a result, Narai became increasingly remote. The village has changed very little over the past fifty years. Narai's picturesque main street, called Naraijuku, is now protected by the government from new development. Among its many attractive old wooden buildings there are two hotels that were built more than 250 years ago. In a country where everything is changing fast, that is very old.

Traditional wooden houses on Narai's main street stand against the village's mountain backdrop.

8

When Japan began developing its industries after World War II, many people left villages in areas like the Kiso Valley to seek jobs in Japan's rapidly developing cities. Today, Narai, like many villages in the Kiso area, is looking increasingly toward tourism to survive.

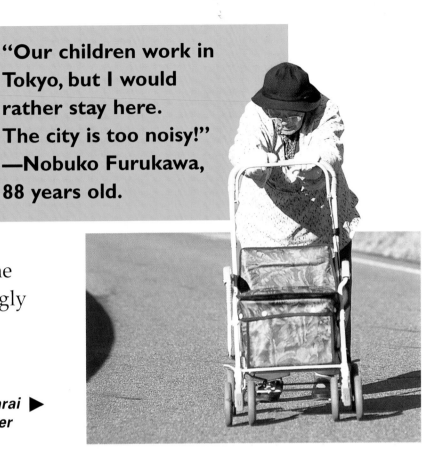

"Our children work in Tokyo, but I would rather stay here. The city is too noisy!"
—Nobuko Furukawa, 88 years old.

More than half of the residents of Narai ▶ are over sixty years old. Most younger people move to the cities.

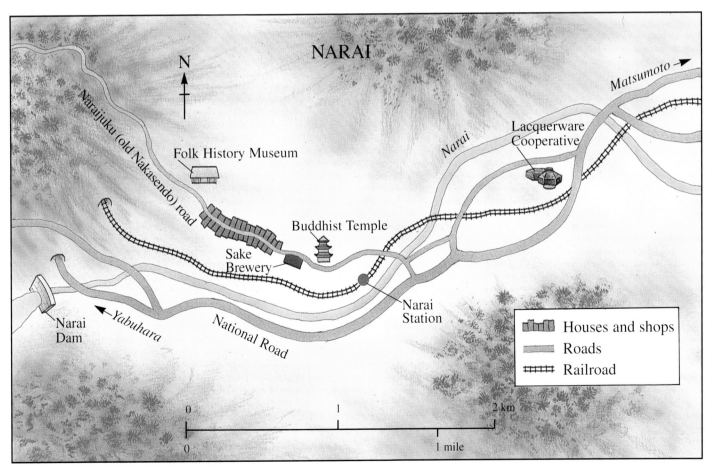

NARAI

N

Matsumoto ▶

Naraijuku (old Nakasendo) road

Folk History Museum

Narai

Lacquerware Cooperative

Buddhist Temple

Sake Brewery

Narai Station

Narai Dam

◀ Yabuhara

National Road

	Houses and shops
	Roads
	Railroad

0   1   2 km

0   1 mile

Landscape and Climate

The dangerously active Mt. Sakurajima, in the south of Kyushu Island.

Japan has four seasons, but since it is a long, narrow chain of islands that stretch more than 1,500 miles, its climate differs from north to south. Conditions in the north are Siberian, with harsh, snowy winters and mild summers. Winters toward the south are gentler, but the summers are very hot and humid. All regions, except the north, have a short rainy season every year from mid-May to mid-June.

JAPAN'S CLIMATE		
	Average temperature	Average annual
	June–August Jan–March	rainfall
Sapporo, Hokkaido:	68°F 23°F	44 inches
Kanazawa, Honshu:	79°F 37°F	102 inches
Tokyo, Pacific Side:	77°F 41°F	55 inches
Okinawa, Riyuku Islands:	82°F 59°F	80 inches

Source: *Facts and Figures Japan* (Foreign Press Center, 1995)

Lying along a fault in the earth's crust, Japan is prone to earthquakes. These can sometimes be devastating, and so far no accurate way has been found to predict them. Where there are earthquakes, there is usually volcanic activity. About one tenth of all the world's active volcanoes are in Japan. Despite the dangers, volcanic activity can be useful. Water heated by molten rock that is deep underground supplies much of the country with hot springs, called *onsen*. Tourist resorts, which have been developed around onsens, are popular for bathing, and the natural hot water is sometimes used for cooking and even for heating homes.

For about three months, from mid-September, coastal Japan is threatened by typhoons. A strong typhoon can cause disastrous floods and landslides by bringing driving rain and hurricane-force winds.

Mountains, many densely forested, occupy 66 percent of the land surface of Japan. They run mainly down through the western side of the islands like a backbone, so the majority of the population live on the flatter land toward the east.

Heavily dependent on imports of raw materials, especially oil, Japan grows enough food to feed itself. However, with the rising cost of home-grown food, Japan is relying increasingly on produce from overseas.

"In 1959 a typhoon blew our roof off. We had to shelter in the local school with the rest of our neighborhood." —Yoshiko Ishihara, resident of Okazaki

The water in Chinoike hot spring, in Kyushu, is colored by the minerals inside it. Chinoike means "pond of blood."

HOT SUMMER PLAINS

Lying on the flat Okazaki plain, where the Yahagi and Oto rivers meet, Okazaki has everything to make it an ideal place to live.

Typical of other towns in the region, Okazaki has both agriculture and industry existing side by side. Rice, soybeans, mushrooms, grapes, and strawberries are cultivated not far from factories that produce cars, machinery, chemicals, knitted goods, and textiles. A good supply of white granite from the nearby Mikawa hills has long made Okazaki famous for its stonecarvers, whose age-old industry is still successful.

A stonecarver in Okazaki making a lantern for decorating a Japanese garden.

Spring in Okazaki finds city parks filled with people picnicking beneath blossoming cherry trees. In the autumn, strollers flock to admire the blazing red Japanese maple trees. The muggy summer sends vacationers to the nearby beaches, and in winter many young people go up to the ski resorts in the mountains in neighboring regions such as Gifu and Nagano.

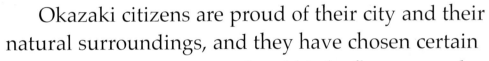

Women in Okazaki Park ▶ have a picnic under the cherry blossoms.

"My class goes out to paint pictures of the cherry blossoms in Okazaki Park. So do schoolchildren from nearly every school in town."—Sachiko Ishihara, 10 years old

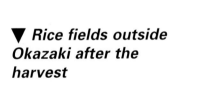

▼ *Rice fields outside Okazaki after the harvest*

Okazaki citizens are proud of their city and their natural surroundings, and they have chosen certain local birds, flowers, and trees as city mascots. Okazaki's bird is the black-and-white Japanese wagtail. Its flower is the lovely purple wisteria blossom. Okazaki's tree is the tall Mikawa black pine, some of which are found along surviving sections of the old Tokaido road.

13

A COOLER VALLEY

The cooler mountain climate of the Kiso Valley means that cherry blossoms come out later in Narai than in Okazaki. It usually snows only on the mountains, but winters can be bitter, with temperatures as low as –4°F. As many a local farmer will tell you, "It's too cold for snow." The farmers of Narai grow rice, vegetables, and fruit, but there are few other natural resources in the Kiso Valley. Although the area is densely wooded, the local forestry industry is in decline. The area's most profitable resource is now its natural beauty. Many hikers and campers visit Narai during the summer, and skiers go to its ski resorts in winter.

Autumn in the Kiso Valley, where the surrounding mountains are among the highest in Japan.

The Kiso Valley's streams and rivers, notably the Kiso River itself, are famous among Japan's many anglers. Several species of freshwater fish are common in the area. Trout, for example, is currently being raised on local fish farms to ensure a plentiful supply. A tributary of the Kiso River, the Narai River flows through Narai and is popular with local anglers.

The Kiso River can flow very fast, especially after rain. Too dangerous for boat transportation, some sections are popular for canoeing, including over the whitewater rapids.

▲ The Narai River, at the bottom of the photo, flows past farmhouses near the village. The farmers' vegetable plots are beside the river.

▲ Narai's landscape is ideal for camping.

"Some years up here it freezes, others I've had my crops flooded. But when I think of summertime, I wouldn't live anywhere else."—Masao Furukuwa, farmer

Home Life

Japanese homes used to have three generations living under one roof, with grandparents living with their children and grandchildren. However, since the 1950s, the growth of crowded cities means that homes are usually only large enough for parents and their children. The average city home for a two-child family has two bedrooms, with a kitchen-dining room and a rather cramped living room. Every household is crammed with high-tech gadgets, including televisions and videos, washing machines, electric rice cookers, and sometimes even heated toilet seats!

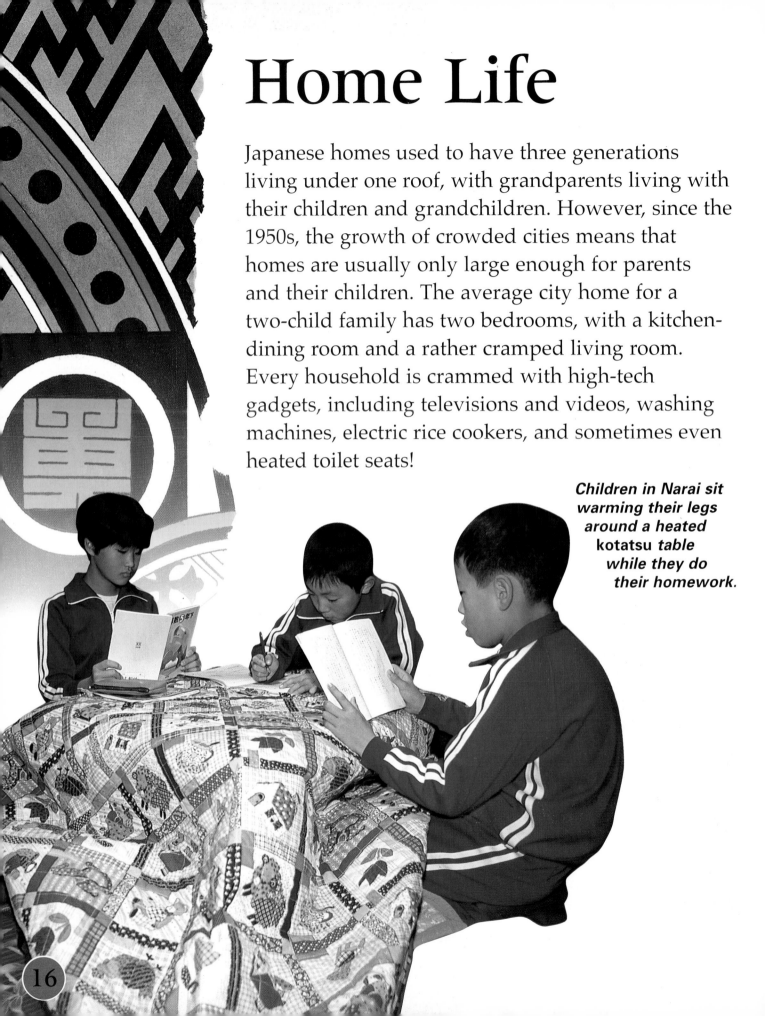

Children in Narai sit warming their legs around a heated kotatsu table while they do their homework.

Yet only newer homes are heated by furnace. Older houses use oil stoves or electric heaters. In winter, many people sit snugly around a low table called a *kotatsu*, which has quilts around the side and a heater underneath.

▲ *A futon bed on* tatami *mat flooring*

The Japanese live at floor level. A traditional floor is covered with smooth, springy matting called *tatami*. People sit at low tables on cushions placed on the tatami floor. Floors are always clean, because no one ever wears shoes at home.

Members of each family take a nightly bath in a square tub filled with piping hot water. However, the bath is just for soaking, not bathing in, because the bathwater is shared. So no one enters the tub without having washed first. Until recently, many households had no baths, and people went to the *sento* (the public bathhouse) instead. The *sento* is still popular today—there's nothing like gossiping with neighbors in a large hot bath!

▼ *An* ofuro, *a traditional Japanese bath. This one is made of fragrant cedar wood.*

Traditional Japanese beds consist of mattresses, called futons, on the floor. These are rolled up in the morning and put away in a cupboard for the day. Futons are still used, but sofas and Western-style beds are now also common.

HOME LIFE IN OKAZAKI

Okazaki has both older houses and modern apartment buildings. In the older houses grandparents, parents, and children often live together, while small families usually live in apartments. Near the car-assembly plant where he works, Kunio Ishihara shares an old house with his wife, mother, and three children.

Every evening, the family eats together around a Western-style kitchen table using chopsticks. Supper always includes rice, pickles, and miso soup, which accompany main dishes of fish or meat. The children also like Western-style food, especially hamburgers, but their grandmother can't even bring herself to taste it. On special occasions, everyone loves to eat *sashimi*, which are delicate mouthfuls of raw fish dipped in soy sauce.

Ten-year-old Sachiko helps her mother clear up, while her father and thirteen-year-old brother Koichi watch television. Eight-year-old Kentaro is upstairs playing computer games, but his mother will soon be up to see that he has done his homework.

"When I was a girl, my father was the boss. But my mother ruled the house and family budget. He used to hand her his monthly pay, and she gave him his pocket money."
—Hiroko Saito, 36 years old

Sachiko and Kentaro eat sushi—small pieces of raw fish rolled with rice inside a leaf of dried seaweed.

Hiroshi Saito's family lives on the ninth floor of an apartment building. Twelve-year-old Harumi and her brother Junichi, nine, wish they saw more of their father, but by the time Hiroshi comes home from work, they are asleep.

Mrs. Saito has a part-time office job, so for supper she saves time by microwaving a supermarket supper. In Japan, men still rule the roost. When Hiroshi comes home, he might expect his wife to put out his *nemaki* (nightclothes) and prepare his bath. Having demanded his supper, he might let her clear up afterward. As in many younger families, however, Hiroshi devotes some of his little free time to sharing household chores.

Sachiko and Kentaro enjoy a quiz program on television. Every Japanese household has at least one television —the bigger the better!

AVERAGE MONEY EACH HOUSEHOLD SPENDS A MONTH

Okazaki:	342,004 yen ($4,155)

Source: *Japan Economic Year Book,* 1995

HOME LIFE IN NARAI

The main street of Narai is lined with old wooden houses. It is so quiet that it looks as though only elderly people and babies live there. During the daytime, most of the villagers work outside the village. Some travel as far as Matsumoto, the area's largest town. Young children are looked after by their grandparents. Many families still live in old wooden farmhouses outside the village. Some houses still have holes in the high ceiling that let out the smoke from the *irori,* a square, sunken, stone fireplace in the living room.

There are few shops along the main village street. Most people in Narai own cars and drive to large nearby supermarkets to do their main shopping and to stock their freezers.

Akio Watanabe is a lacquerware craftsman who lives on the main village street. Akio lives in a house he shares with his parents, his wife, his ten-year-old son Yoshi, and his twelve-year-old daughter Naoko. Supper in Narai is not quite the same as in Okazaki. Local river fish is available, which, in the Watanabe household, is caught by Yoshi and his father over the weekend. In season, there are

"It's not always easy living in an old wooden house like ours. We have a lot of repairs, and our heating bills are high."
—Akio Watanabe, lacquerware craftsman

▼ *Children warm themselves in front of an* irori *fireplace. The kettle is set to boil for tea.*

Old shop fronts along Naraijuku, the main street in Narai. These shops have been recently restored to look like they did a century ago.

sometimes stews of wild boar. There are also often dishes of mountain potatoes and vegetables grown by a local farmer.

The farmer, Mr. Furukawa, lives with his wife in the farmhouse his grandfather was born in. They have a state pension that they add to by growing vegetables. Now grown up, the Furukawas' children left for Tokyo thirty years ago, during the late sixties. Life is more comfortable—but lonelier—for the Furukawas than when they were young. They look forward to family visits in summer and at New Year, when they hear all about a city world they have seen only on television.

AVERAGE MONEY EACH HOUSEHOLD SPENDS A MONTH	
Narai:	327,456 yen ($3,795)

Source: *Japan Economic Year Book*, 1995

Japan at Work

Take a look around you. How many things can you see that say "Made in Japan"? You will probably find a computer, stereo, compact disc-player, video, television, or tape deck that is Japanese. Someone in your house may own a Japanese watch or camera, or play a musical instrument made in Japan, or have a car that is Japanese. If you play computer games, the hardware and software might be Japanese. All these high-tech industries employ many Japanese workers. Other giant industries in Japan include steel, heavy machinery, chemical, and shipbuilding. Nearly all the electronics goods made around the world today contain some Japanese parts.

High-tech machinery in a factory in northern Kyushu. Many large Japanese factories now use robots, which often do the work of humans.

▲ *Office workers on their way to work in Tokyo*

WORK IN JAPAN	
Type of work	(percentage of population)
Agriculture:	6
Manufacturing:	33.9
Services:	60.1
Average working hours per week:	36.8
Average working hours per year:	1,913 (one week's paid holiday)

Source: *Facts and Figures Japan*
(Foreign Press Center, 1995)

The success of Japanese goods worldwide is due to sheer hard work. Until recently, working long hours six days a week was regarded as normal by Japanese workers. One of the results of too much work, however, is too much production. During the 1980s, the Japanese government started to reduce working hours, so most big companies now work five days a week. However, smaller companies still often work long daily hours, and give only one day off.

Since many small manufacturing companies depend on larger ones for their livelihood, they compete fiercely with one another for business. Such small factories are often called sweatshops. Workers flocking to Japan from poorer countries are often employed either in these or in the construction industry.

Meanwhile, the position of women in Japan's workforce is very different from other industrialized countries. About a third of working women only work part-time, and only very few become managers.

◀ *A man using a tractor to plant rice seedlings, a job that used to be done by hand*

23

WORK IN OKAZAKI

Okazaki is a center for textile, car, machinery, and chemical production, but it is also famous for traditional crafts that are centuries old. These products include painted festival banners, fireworks, and the carved wooden Buddhist altars that are found in most Japanese homes. Stonecarving, especially garden ornaments, is another traditional industry in which Okazaki leads Japan. Another famous traditional product is miso, a nourishing soybean paste used in soups and seasonings. Since Okazaki is also a farming area, it is not unusual to see rice paddies alongside apartment buildings. Most people in Okazaki, whatever type of work they do, work long hours. Office workers, like Hiroshi Saito, usually work until at least 9:00 P.M. Saito has an hour's journey to work every day, so that by the time he gets home, about 10:00 P.M., his children are asleep. But working hours are getting shorter, and now Saito only has to work every other Saturday.

A modern miso factory. Miso paste has been made in Okazaki for centuries.

Mr. Ishihara is a foreman in a car-assembly plant. Ishihara believes he is lucky to have a forty-hour work week because it means that he gets home in time to have supper with his family. Like most Japanese firms, Ishihara's company is organized so that there are senior and junior workers.

People who work in companies in Okazaki, as elsewhere in Japan, are promoted according to their age rather than their ability. They can expect employment for their entire working life. Larger companies provide many benefits, often including housing. In return, they expect a worker's complete loyalty. This sometimes means working overtime with no extra pay. These days, however, layoffs are becoming more frequent in Japan. In a solid company like his, Mr. Ishihara is secure. But in many companies, the old "lifetime employment system" is disappearing.

"My dad makes cars. When I grow up, I'm going to work in a company making computer games."
—Kentaro Ishihara, 8 years old

▼ A banner being painted for a holiday such as Boys' Day

25

WORK IN NARAI

In the past, the forests around Narai, which belong to the Japanese government, provided employment for thousands of workers. But as the demand for timber grew, Japan began importing cheaper wood from abroad, so the livelihoods of many people in forested areas like Narai dwindled.

This lumberyard in the Kiso Valley has lost much work because cheaper wood is being imported.

The Kiso forests are famous for *hinoki* (Japanese cedar) trees. These trees are sacred to the Japanese, so they are cut down to build Shinto shrines and to make a variety of local wooden products. Another craft using local types of wood is Japanese lacquer.

Mr. Watanabe is one of several lacquer craftsmen in Narai. Lacquer is a varnish, usually red or black, with a very high gloss. The lacquering process is painstakingly slow and careful, since the gleaming surface must be perfect. Mr. Watanabe learned his craft from his father and now produces trays, boxes, and bowls. He belongs to a lacquerware cooperative that groups craftsmen together. The goods are distributed to shops around Japan, and the craftsmen share the profits.

In agriculture, the Narai area shares the same problems as Japan in general. Out of the 4 million people still working on farms, 63 percent are over 55 years old. Mr. Furukawa and his wife, who are 65 and 68 years old, are typical of local farmers. Their children chose more secure jobs in the city rather than continuing the family tradition of farming. Although some of their neighbors still cultivate rice, the Furukawas gave it up to concentrate on the growth of *sansai,* or mountain vegetables. They also grow *kaki* (persimmon fruit) trees and sell the dried fruit to local shops and supermarkets. Every winter, the Furukawas hang strings of bright orange *kaki* to dry on the eaves of their old wooden farmhouse.

"A lot of my friends want to work in the city when they grow up. Not me. I want to stay and be a craftsman like my father."
—Yoshi Watanabe, 10 years old

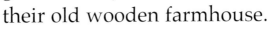

◄▲ *Freshly painted lacquer bowls in a Narai workshop. To ensure an even coat, craftsmen use a special brush, tipped with human hair.*

Going to School

All Japanese children must go to school between the ages of six and fifteen. Most begin at four years old at nursery school. Starting elementary school at six, they then enter junior high school when they are twelve. At fifteen, more than 90 percent go to senior high school for four years. After this, about one third will go on to university and training colleges. The fierce competition to enter senior schools and universities, however, is a serious problem in Japan's education system. Children have to pass entrance examinations with extremely high scores. Even some nursery schools require three year olds to take and pass entrance tests.

When exams draw near, pupils' workloads increase dramatically. Most attend *juku* (cram school) for about two hours after normal school and then have too much homework for a good night's sleep. The Japanese call this "examination hell." Complaints about children's workloads recently, however, have meant that the amount of pressure on children in the education system is beginning to drop.

A boy practicing the art of calligraphy to improve his handwriting

"These days, school kids have to work, work, work. With all that education, they hardly go outdoors anymore."
—Masao Furukawa, 72 years old

Schools still have time for music, arts, and crafts as well as games, swimming, and athletics. Japan is famous for martial arts, and most schoolchildren, including girls, practice some form of martial arts at school. Martial arts are taught to encourage self-discipline.

Japanese children learn to fend for themselves at a young age. Elementary pupils travel to school on their own, while children under six are escorted by elder children. The school system in Japan produces very high standards of education, and Japanese schoolchildren achieve the highest standards in the world in math and science. They show great enthusiasm for learning, and truancy from school is very rare.

A young rugby player and his coach in Okazaki. Like soccer, rugby has become very popular in Japan over the past ten years.

AFTER-CLASS ACTIVITIES	
	Pupils who take part in activities
Watching television	75.6%
Reading magazines and comics	64.2%
Outdoor sports	42.4%
Listening to music	34.4%
Reading books	27.5%
Hobbies	26.2%

Source: *Facts and Figures Japan* (Foreign Press Center, 1995)

SCHOOL IN OKAZAKI

Okazaki has plenty of schools, from nursery level right through college level. Kunio Ishihara's children go to schools near their home. Wearing white cotton sun-hats and bright-red schoolbags on their backs, like most elementary school pupils, Sachiko and Kentaro catch the bus each morning at 8:30 A.M. Unlike their elder brother Koichi, they don't wear uniforms yet. Koichi wears the standard dark blue uniform of pupils at high school, which is modeled on German naval-academy uniforms of the nineteenth century. The jacket of the girls' uniform has a sailor collar with white edges.

Koichi cycles to Kozan Junior High School, which has its own bicycle racks. Like his younger brother and sister, he goes on many school outings to local factories, museums, and places of interest. Every summer, both elementary and junior high school pupils go on school trips, which include camping.

Girls discuss electronics at Kozan Junior High School in Okazaki.

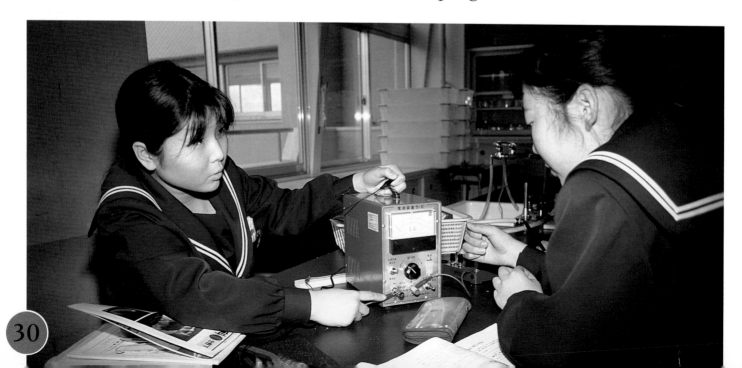

◀ *Kendo is a martial art based on samurai sword skills. It is practiced by both boys and girls at Kozan Junior High School.*

Koichi likes baseball very much, a sport played in schools all over the country. In Japan, boys play baseball and girls play volleyball. The best players are singled out to join teams that compete in national finals. Koichi also learns kendo, a martial art based on samurai sword skills. His school runs a wide range of *kurabu* (clubs) to allow pupils to pursue hobbies and activities after school.

The school's pupils are responsible for tidying their own classrooms every day and also for giving the whole school a thorough cleaning once a month. This teaches them to work together as a team, which is considered very important in Japan.

▼ *The main building of Kozan Junior High School in Okazaki*

"Western kids are luckier than us. We have to use Chinese characters. No wonder we have to work so hard at school!"
—Koichi Ishihara, 13 years old

31

SCHOOL IN NARAI

The only school in Narai is an elementary school. This means that high-school pupils have to take a train to the nearby town of Yabuhara. Some senior high school students may have to travel farther along the line as far as Matsumoto, the area's largest town. They usually cycle to Narai station and leave their bicycles in a specially provided parking area. Nowhere in Japan is too far from a school for a child to get to, which is why 90 percent of the population was able to read and write as long ago as 1912. Children from a village without a high school, like Narai, simply travel somewhere that has one.

▲ *Off to school early in the morning in Narai. All pupils cycling to school have to wear white crash helmets.*

▼ *Pupils from Narai on a school outing to the great hall of Todaiji temple, in Nara*

▲ *Pupils discussing a geometry project at Narai Elementary School*

There is little difference between the programs of the schools in Narai and Yabuhara and the schools in Okazaki. Children from Narai, however, such as Naoko Watanabe, may have more trouble in finding a cram school when they need one than children from Okazaki. Naoko Watanabe will soon be starting junior high school and is about to take the entrance examination. To prepare for the exam, Naoko is tutored a few hours a week at her home by a local teacher.

The choice of after-school club activities is more limited in Narai than in Okazaki, but a new soccer club has just started, which Naoko's brother, Yoshi, is looking forward to joining. Soccer has recently become a craze in Japan. The village school also arranges outings for pupils. The Watanabe children are looking forward to a school bus trip this spring, when they will be taken to see the great temples of Nara and Kyoto.

"What I like best at school is baseball. If I practice hard, one day I'll be in the national high school finals."
—Yoshi Watanabe, 10 years old

Japan at Play

FAVORITE HOBBIES AND ACTIVITIES

	Percentage of adults who take part in activities
Watching videos	44.5
Music (radio, tapes, CDs)	41.7
Gardening	33.2
Going to the movies	30.1
Video games	28.7
Pachinko	28.1
Going to concerts	22
Watching sports	20.7
Weaving, knitting, needlecraft	17.4
Do-it-yourself, carpentry	15.4

Source: *White Paper on Leisure*, Japanese Leisure Development Center, 1993

As working hours are gradually being reduced, the Japanese have more leisure time than ever before.

Almost every household has a radio and at least one television. The Japanese are avid readers and often read on the train to work. Large numbers of books are published every year, but they are exceeded by the number of magazines. Comics are more popular in Japan than anywhere else in the world, with millions of copies sold every week.

The Japanese are enthusiastic tourists, at home and abroad. Every weekend, millions go on outings, sightseeing, and picnics.

Karaoke is a Japanese invention, which is often part of an outing or even a wedding. Another popular pastime is *pachinko*, an upright pinball game played in special arcades.

◀ *Spectators at a baseball game*

Every Japanese city has a baseball stadium. Baseball, called yakkyu, *has been Japan's national sport since the 1900s.*

The Japanese are also very fond of theme parks, such as Tokyo Disneyland, which attracts millions of visitors every year.

Trips to the movies remain very popular, although televisions and videos have taken away some of the audiences.

Sports and athletics are very popular, both to watch and to take part in. Sumo is a unique and traditional form of Japanese wrestling that dates back a thousand years and features heavy-weight opponents. Although expensive, tickets for Tokyo's national sumo tournaments sell out months in advance. Many sumo fans are happy to see tournaments on television. Baseball, which was introduced from the United States at the end of the nineteenth century, is Japan's national sport. Another popular sport, which has seen a sudden and fantastic rise in popularity during the 1990s, is soccer.

LEISURE TIME IN OKAZAKI

Most people in Okazaki like to get out of the city on weekends and on holidays. Many families, like the Ishihara family, enjoy driving out to the nearby Mikawa Hills. They often have lunch there with relatives in a scenic restaurant. There is also a popular *onsen* hotel in the hills, where the Ishihara family spends a couple of days over New Year. This summer, the family is going to take a week's vacation on the island of Shikoku, where they will stay in a beach resort.

"My hobby is pottery. My pot in the Okazaki Children's Arts Museum won a prize."
—Junichi Saito, 12 years old

◀ Junichi Saito practicing his pottery at the Children's Art Museum.

▲ The Children's Art Museum in Okazaki, where children can do pottery, painting, and many other crafts.

CLOTHES WORN IN OKAZAKI

Leisure time:	Casual clothes, tracksuits, jeans, running shoes. Some emphasis on fashion. *Yukata* (cotton kimono) worn by both men and women at summer festivals.
Formal occasions:	Kimono or Western formal wear for both men and women

Although few people have gardens in Okazaki, many people like to shape *bonsai* trees, which are miniature trees. Bonsai trees are kept about 1½ feet high, and they must be carefully cut and wired to stunt their growth.

Traditional arts are also popular in Okazaki. On Saturdays, after she has dropped off the children at the sports center, Mrs. Ishihara takes lessons on the samisen, a long-necked, three-stringed guitar.

Young people in Okazaki like both foreign and Japanese rock and pop music. Dance clubs are popular in the city, although many drive to Nagoya for a bigger choice of clubs. Their parents mostly prefer *enka*—a type of folk music that is well-suited for karaoke singing.

There are nineteen annual festivals in Okazaki, mostly connected to shrines, the Shinto places of worship. By far the most exciting is the Summer Festival in August, for which the townspeople turn up. In addition to colorful parades and costumed dancing, the events reach a climax with a fireworks display over the Sugo River. With fireworks from Okazaki's famous Mikawa workshops, the display is the most spectacular in Japan.

This Shinto festival is called Shichi-go-san, which means "seven-five-three." Children of these ages dress in their best clothes for blessings at shrines.

LEISURE TIME IN NARAI

In both Narai and Okazaki, as in villages and cities all over Japan, the Japanese are devoted television fans. In Narai, the Watanabes' television is always turned on, even though no one seems to be watching it much of the time. Yoshi Watanabe never misses a moment of the hour's cartoon programs when he comes home from school.

Life in Narai is so quiet that you can hear the Narai River from the main street. People looking for social entertainment have to go to Yabuhara, or even Matsumoto, to find restaurants or bars.

Children in Narai often take part in after-school activities, such as gymnastics classes, soccer, or baseball. Computer games are also very popular.

Unlike city kids, the Watanabe children don't have to go very far for angling, hiking, camping, or skiing in the winter. But their biggest thrill is their summer trip to Tokyo Disneyland.

▼ *Hiking and camping are popular in the mountains and forests of Kiso.*

"What I like best on Sunday is when my dad takes me fishing. He gets quite annoyed if my fish are bigger than his!"—Yoshi Watanabe, 10 years old

38

Kiso ponies, which ▶ used to be the only form of transportation around Narai, are still raised in the area.

In the summer, the children of Narai, like many Japanese children, collect insects. They especially like collecting large, horned rhinoceros beetles and *semi*, the noisy Japanese cricket. The children put them in special clear plastic boxes, where they keep them as pets, feeding them bits of watermelon.

In the summer elderly people in Narai are often visited by their children and grandchildren, who live in the cities. The Furukawa grandchildren look to their grandfather as an authority on insects. He takes them to see fireflies, which are mostly gone from Japan's polluted cities. Another holiday highlight is when they visit a relative who raises Kiso ponies in the hills. These small, hardy ponies, golden brown with black manes and tails, used to be the only means of transportation in the region. Now they are brought out during festival pageants in the Kiso area, and the Furukawa children ride them around the paddock.

CLOTHES WORN IN NARAI	
Leisure time:	Casual clothes, tracksuits, jeans, running shoes. No emphasis on fashion. *Yukata* (cotton kimono) worn at summer festivals.
Formal occasions:	Kimono worn by nearly all women. Kimono or Western formal wear for men.

39

The Future

After World War II, millions of Japanese left the countryside to work in the cities. Many cities, like Tokyo, grew too large too quickly. As a result, many Japanese now live in cramped homes, so their standard of living is fairly low.

To create more space, many cities are now constructing high-rise buildings, which are changing the appearance of Japanese cities. It may be sad that so many attractive old buildings are disappearing in Japan, but many have been destroyed by earthquakes. For example, Kobe's older districts were destroyed in the terrible earthquake of 1995, and in the Tokyo-Yokohama area another devastating earthquake could happen at any moment. To reduce future damage, the Japanese now use earthquake-proof steel and concrete for new buildings.

On January 17, 1995, whole districts of Kobe were destroyed by the most serious earthquake in Japan since 1923. More than 5,000 people died.

Japan's future is bright, but its boom years are over. Its manufactured goods are more expensive, so exports have fallen. Japan also now has to compete with other rapidly industrializing countries around the Pacific. But the country looks set to remain the world's leader in science and technology, and Japan is working on advances in computers and in bioengineering.

Skyscrapers in Tokyo are designed to resist earthquakes.

There are plans to reduce the Japanese work week to forty hours, which will boost Japan's leisure industry. However, falling exports mean that unemployment is rising. In addition, robots are taking over assembly tasks in many Japanese factories. If too many factories use robots, many workers could be replaced by machines.

Becoming a world leader in only fifty years has, however, caused environmental damage. Major disasters in the past have made Japan take better care of pollution. The control of gas and fuel emissions is now very strict, and much has been done to ensure a cleaner future.

MAJOR EARTHQUAKES			
DATE	PLACE	DEATHS	STRENGTH (Richter scale)
Sept. 23, 1923	Tokyo	100,000+	no record
Dec. 21, 1946	Honshu	2,000	8.4
June 28, 1948	Fukui	5,131	7.3
May 26, 1983	N. Honshu	81	7.7
July 12, 1993	Hokkaido	200+	7.7
Jan. 17, 1995	Kobe	5,400+	7.2

Source: *Facts and Figures Japan* (Foreign Press Center, 1995)

THE FUTURE OF OKAZAKI

Okazaki is a thriving city that looks set to continue to grow in both wealth and population. Recently, a sharp increase in immigrant factory workers, particularly from South America and the Philippines, is making the city more international. Plans for the city include another city center around the train station, and a new Okazaki Central Park, which will include facilities for culture, leisure, and sports. Other major works include a new city hospital, a community welfare center, and a vast welfare building serving the whole region. Okazaki has also been chosen by the government as a base for a new multi-media network. This will be housed in a giant center for local information and communications.

Two children from Umezono elementary school in Okazaki

42

Okazaki's environment, like many other Japanese cities, has suffered from the city's growth. In Gamagori, once Okazaki's local beach resort, industrial waste made the water unsafe for swimming, and during the early 1970s the beach had to be buried under a concrete seafront. However, Okazaki's citizens now put different kinds of garbage out on different days, so that metal, glass, burnable, and nonburnable garbage are separated. Cans and glass are collected for recycling, which is considered vital throughout Japan. To recycle some of the glass, Okazaki's city council even runs a glass-blowing workshop, which is open to everyone.

▲ *Members of the Okazaki fire department practice a fire drill.*

◀ *The concrete promenade of Gamagori, Okazaki's local beach resort, which was created after pollution ruined the original beach*

THE FUTURE OF NARAI

Thanks to efforts made to preserve its scenic beauty, Narai's future as a tourist attraction is quite safe, and its popularity has increased during the past few years. A very old *sake* (Japanese rice wine) brewery along the main street has become a national landmark, and the village's few businesses now include souvenir shops.

Apart from tourism, Narai's future is less certain. Japanese farmers have suffered from the growing amount of cheaper imports from abroad, especially since 1990, when the country's booming economy slowed. Small shops like Narai's grocery, for example, are being increasingly threatened by large supermarkets. Some of these are importing goods from abroad and selling them at rock-bottom prices.

▼ ▶ *A craftsman makes traditional wooden combs in the Kiso village museum.*

As communications and technology become more advanced, an increasing number of children will probably return to villages like Narai in the future.

Lacquerware production still thrives in Narai, but many other old crafts are dying out. The government is trying to preserve these traditional crafts, mainly by having older craftsmen working in museums. In the Kiso area, such crafts include the hand tooling of wooden combs.

Local authorities near Narai have recently tried to attract people back from the cities by offering them attractive housing deals. So while many country people have left for the cities, city people are gradually moving to the country. The development of computer communications will soon make living and working in remoter areas much easier than before. In the future, many more people will want to live in villages like Narai.

Glossary

Active volcano   A volcano that is likely to erupt.

Angler   Someone who fishes with a rod and line.

Calligraphy   The practice of handwriting as an art. The Japanese often hang large-lettered works of calligraphy, often poems, on the wall.

Fault   A crack in the earth.

Hardware   Equipment and machinery. Computer hardware refers to the computer itself and the printer, as well as any other equipment that makes up the system.

Industrialized   Referring to a country where the economy is mainly based on manufacturing and business.

Kimono   A loose robe with wide sleeves and a broad sash.

Kurabu   From the English word "club." Many modern Japanese words like this are of foreign, usually English, origin.

Manufacturing   The production of goods.

Matsuri   A Japanese religious festival.

Onsen   A Japanese word meaning "hot spring." In volcanic areas in Japan, water sometimes comes naturally heated out of the ground.

Produce   Crops; fruit, vegetables, and foodstuffs produced from agriculture.

Resource   Whatever the land has that people need to live and to make money. Water, wood, coal, and minerals are all resources.

Richter scale   A scale used for measuring earthquakes. Level three on the scale is strong enough to be felt, whereas level seven can topple buildings. The highest earthquake ever recorded measured 8.9 on the Richter scale.

Samurai   Japanese warriors from medieval times. The samurai ruled Japan until 1868.

Services   Work such as tourism and banking, which does not make goods but supplies people with services they need.

Software   The programs a computer needs to make it work. Computer games are software.

Textiles   Materials used for making clothing. Cotton, wool, silk, and artificial fibers such as lycra are all textiles.

Tributary   A river or stream that feeds a bigger river.

Typhoon   A storm with high winds and a great deal of rain. Typhoons occur in the China Sea and the Eastern Pacific down to the Philippines. They can often be disastrous.

Volcanic   Having to do with volcanoes.

White-water rapids   Rocks on the riverbed form small waterfalls called rapids. Since the water can flow very fast in rapids, it becomes white with foam.

Yukata   A cotton kimono worn in the summer.

Further Information

Books to Read

Department of Geography Staff. *Japan in Pictures*. Visual Geography Series. Minneapolis: Lerner Publications, 1989.

Downer, Lesley. *Japan*. Modern Industrial World. New York: Thomson Learning, 1994.

Flint, David. *Islands of the Pacific Rim and Their People*. People and Places. New York: Thomson Learning, 1994.

Hoobler, Dorothy and Hoobler, Thomas. *Showa: The Age of Hirohito*. New York: Walker & Co., 1990.

Kitano, Harry. *Japanese Americans*. The Peoples of North America. New York: Chelsea House, 1987.

O'Toole, Thomas. *Global Economics*. Economics for Today. Minneapolis: Lerner Publications, 1994.

Ridgewell, Jenny. *A Taste of Japan*. Food Around the World. New York: Thomson Learning, 1994.

Stefoff, Rebecca. *Japan*. Places and Peoples of the World. New York: Chelsea House, 1988.

Tames, Richard. *Japan Since 1945*. North Pomfret, VT: Trafalgar Square, 1989.

Useful Address

Japanese Embassy, 2520 Massachusetts Avenue NW, Washington, D. C. 20008

VIDEOS

Empire of the Sun (1987) The story of an English boy living in Japanese-occupied Shanghai in the 1930s. When World War II breaks out, he is separated from his parents and held prisoner by the Japanese.

The Seven Samurai (1954) The adventure of seven samurai warriors in sixteenth-century Japan, who agree to defend a peasant village. One of the many movies available from acclaimed Japanese director Akira Kurosawa.

Tampopo (1987) Eccentric Japanese comedy about a woman who desires to create the best noodle bar in Japan.

PICTURE ACKNOWLEDGMENTS

All photographs are by Jim Holmes, of Axiom Photographic Agency.

All map artwork is by Peter Bull.

Index

Page numbers in **bold** refer to photographs.

agriculture 12, 27

baseball 35, **35**
beaches **1**, 12, 36, 43, **43**
Buddhism 4

cherry blossoms **4**, 12, 13, **13**, 14
civil war 6
climate 10–15
computers 18, 22, 25, 38, 41, 45

earthquakes 11, 40, **40**
employment 9
environment 41, 43
exporting 41

family 16, 17, 18, **18**, 19, 20, 21
farming 4, 12, 14, 21, 27, 44
  rice 4, 12, 14, 24, 27
festivals 5, 37, **37**, 39
fishing 15, 20, 38
food 11, 18, 21
forestry 14, 26, **26**
futons 17, **17**

immigrants 23, 42
importing 11, 44
industry 5, 7, 9, 12, 22, **22**, 23, 24, 40, 41
  car production 5, 12, 18, 22, 24, **25**, 25
  chemical 12, 22, 24
  computer 22
  electronics 5, 22, 41
  textiles 12. 24, 46

Karaoke 34, 37

layoffs 25

martial arts 29, 31, **31**
mountains 8, 11, 12, 14, **38**

Narai 8–9, 14, 27, 39
  future 44–45
  home life 20–21
  leisure time 38–39
  schools 32–33
  work 26–27

Okazaki 6–7, 13
  future 42–43
  home life 18–19
  leisure time 36–37, 42
  schools 30–31
  work 24–25

pachinko 34
paddy fields **13**, 24
pollution 41, **44**
population 7, 8, 11, 32, 42

railroads 8
religion 4
restaurants 36
rivers
  Kiso 15
  Narakawa 15, 38
  Oto 12
  Sugo 37
  Yahagi 12
roads 6, 8, 13

school 28–33
science and technology 41
seasons 10
settlers 4
Shinto 4, 5, 5, 37
Shoguns 6
shopping 20, **21**
sport 29, 33, **34**, 35, **35**, 38
sumo wrestling 35
supermarkets 20, 44
sushi **18**
sweatshops 23

television 16, **19**, 21, 22, 34, 35, 38
temples 7, **32**, 33
Tokyo 4, 9, 6, 19, 21, 38, 40
tourism 9, 11, 12, 14, 34, 44
typhoons 11, 46

unemployment 25, 41
United States 5
university 28

vacations 36
volcanoes **3**, **10**, 11, 46

World War II 5, 9, 40